CANDY LAND

Lord Licorice
A Picture Clue Story

ISBN 0-439-32180-8

12 11 10 9 8 7 6 5 4 3 2 1   1 2 3 4 5 6/0

Illustrated by Ken Edwards
Designed by Peter Koblish

Printed in the U.S.A.
First Scholastic printing, November 2001

CANDY LAND®
Lord Licorice
A Picture Clue Story

by Jackie Glassman
Illustrated by Ken Edwards

SCHOLASTIC INC.

New York   Toronto   London   Auckland   Sydney   Mexico City   New Delhi   Hong Kong   Buenos Aires

One day in Candy Land, said to , , and , "This is too small for all of us. You need to build a of your own."

"Build your strong," warned ,
"so that you will be safe from ."

decided to build a out of .

One day came and knocked on the . " , oh , let me come in!"

"No, no, I won't let you in, not by the sugar on my chinny-chin-chin."

"Well," said 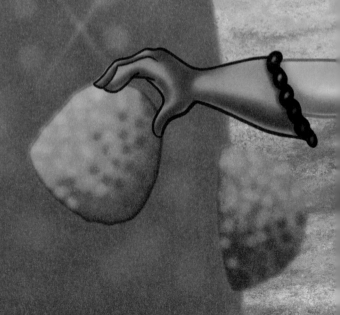, "then I'll chew and I'll chew and I'll eat your 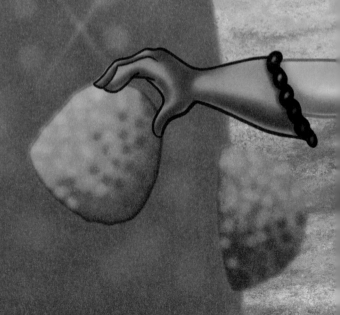 up." So he chewed and he chewed and he ate the 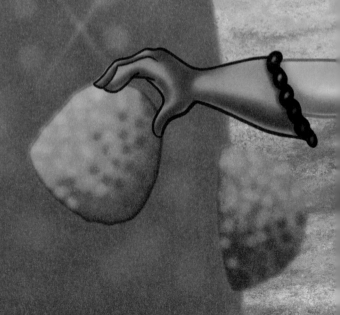 up.

"Yikes!" screamed 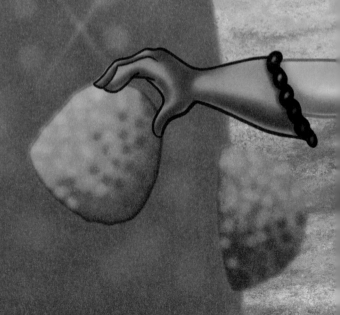 as he ran away to find 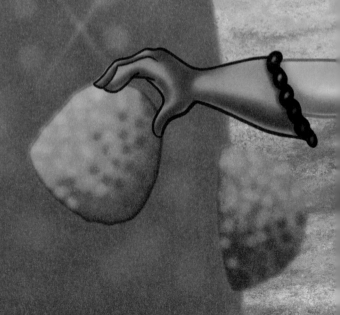 .

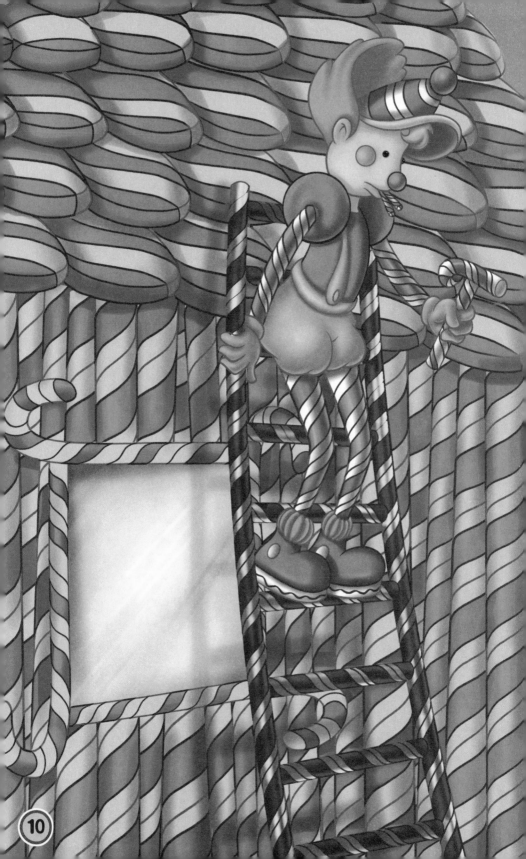

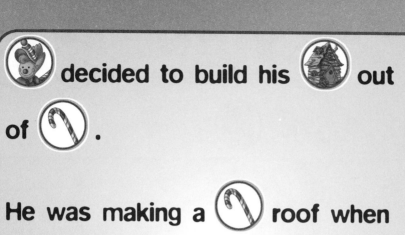 decided to build his out of .

He was making a roof when came running up.

" has eaten my   !" cried .

and went inside the

and locked the .

12

But soon, came knocking at the 🪟. "🐻, oh 🐻, let me come in!"

"No, no, I won't let you in, not by the mint on my chinny-chin-chin."

"Then I'll crunch and I'll crunch . . . *burp* . . . and I'll eat your  up!" yelled  .

So he crunched and he crunched and he ate the  up until his belly was very full and starting to hurt.

On the shore of Ice Cream Sea,
was putting the final touches on her
  when up ran and .

"What's wrong?" asked when she
saw their scared faces.

and told all about

 eating up their s.

"If we hadn't run away, he would have eaten us up, too!" exclaimed  .

But  wasn't scared.

She invited them in for 🍦. But, just

as they were about to eat, there was

a knock at the 🚪.

", oh , let me come in!" demanded .

"Go away, silly old !" yelled back .

 and  looked at her in amazement.

23

Now was really angry.

"I'll lick and I'll lick . . ." growled .

But he could not finish his words

because with each lick of the

, his belly hurt more and grew

bigger and rounder.

Finally, when he could eat no more,  fell to the ground and rolled down the hill. *Splash* he went, falling into the freezing-cold sea. From the , the three friends watched  run from the sea with  dripping from his nose.

"Hooray!" cheered , , and .

Then 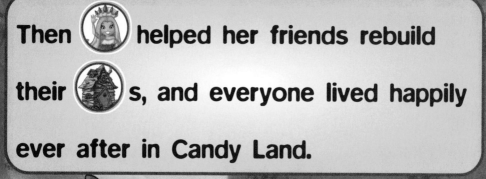 helped her friends rebuild their s, and everyone lived happily ever after in Candy Land.

Did you spot all the picture clues in this Candy Land story?

Each picture clue is on a flash card. Ask a grown-up to cut out the flash cards. Then try reading the words on the back of the cards. The pictures will be your clue.

Have fun!

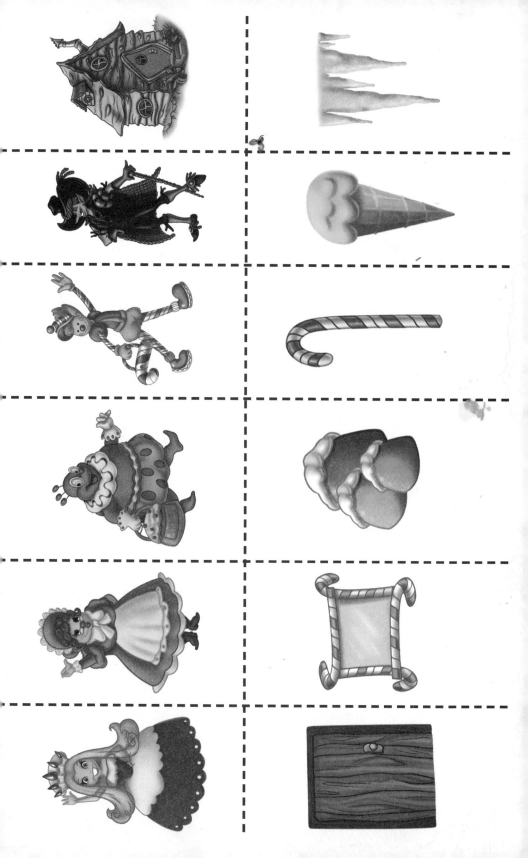

house

Lord
Licorice

Mr. Mint

Jolly

Gramma Nutt

Queen
Frostine

icicles

ice cream

candy cane

gumdrop

window

door